# i'M SeRIOuS.


## By


## Wally DiCioccio, Jr.

ISBN: 1-4140-1322-1 (e-book)
ISBN: 1-4140-1321-3 (Paperback)

This book is printed on acid free paper.

1stBooks - rev.11/10/03

To my wonderful siblings Mike and Rosanna, and my also wonderful parents Luisa and Wally, who made me realize I'm a funny guy. To Jerry, Jim, Adam, Rodney, Leslie, Rowan, George, Harland, Bill, Dave, Curley, Larry, and Moe for inspiring me. And to Grandpa DiCioccio for teaching me to use my voice in order to make a difference.

# Acknowledgements

I'd like to thank my family and friends for their support. In particular, I'd like to thank my pals, Mark Cencora and Jenn Penksa for inspiring some of my jokes/stories. I'd also like to thank Diane Wilson, Mark Marinaccio, Craig Harrison, Dawn Klubeck, and Will Seychew for believing in me every step of the way.

Finally, I would like to thank my photographer, Brian K. McMillen.

BKM Photography
910 Main St.
Buffalo, NY 14202
(716) 875-1035

## Intro

When I was seventeen, my brother, Mike introduced me to the work of Jerry Seinfeld. Along with many others, Seinfeld was a huge inspiration. I have always believed that my ultimate purpose in life is to entertain people and make them laugh. Soon after reading one of Seinfeld's books my grandpa Benny passed away. He taught me that if I ever wanted to make an impact I have to use my voice. While clearing out my grandpa's house, my dad found a blank black notebook. He didn't find a use for it so he asked me if I wanted it. I accepted it, not really knowing what I would use it for. I was just sure it would become handy someday. I then began jotting funny stories and thoughts in it. I would write a little bit each night before bed and eventually I filled the whole notebook. I'm going onto my third notebook and I'm sure there will be many more to come. Sometimes I stay up all night because ideas just keep coming to me. Other nights it can be quite difficult to come up with anything at all.

This book is loaded with funny ideas but you have to provide the delivery and performance. If any part of it confuses you, just move on to the next part. Enjoy!

## The Early Days

I was born in the early 80's and when I was a baby I was afraid of everything. I was even afraid of my own shadow. I was always getting sick. I'd get earaches like it was my job. I would drink milk, sit in a crib, and hangout with a stuffed Kermit the Frog all day. I just wanted to sit around and chew on stuff. The old ladies enjoyed playing with my feet and trying to make me laugh. Then when they'd change my diapers I'd wiz all over their blouses. I was a fat baby. I looked like I swallowed Winnie the Pooh.

I really miss being a kid. Such simple things amused me, like balloons. If you were to hand me a balloon today, I'd probably tell you to bite me. I wasn't exactly the sharpest knife in the drawer though. I'm still not. My older sister was smarter, so I was always compared to her. Unlike the Ghostbusters, I *was* afraid of ghosts. I was afraid of everything. I would eat carrots to be like Bugs Bunny, I ate spinach to be strong like Popeye, I ate pizza like the Turtles, and I got a hernia from trying to lift a man-hole cover. That was believable though, four smart talking turtles learn karate from a talking rat. His name was Splinter. He was old and wise. I find it funny how he is named after the smallest grain of wood visible to the naked eye. Do the Turtle creators have an inside joke here? Are they trying to say that the old rat isn't getting any action at the Mickey Mouse Club? Lace that guy's cheese pizza with some Viagra!

Cartoons were what I watched. Didn't we all? I still do. Have you ever been so annoyed that you just felt like painting a hole on the wall and running away? One of my favorite cartoons was Pinocchio. Man, if I were him I'd be a big liar too. The dude's best friend is a top hat wearing cricket, and he lives with a silly old man. The kids at school must have made fun of him all of the time.

-" *Hey Pinocchio, who's that little guy you were hanging out with yesterday?"*

- *"Oh, um...that was my little buddy Jim. He's pretty cool. He gives me good advice. He's a...ummm...he's a finger puppet. We met at a puppet show. He wanted me to teach him the ropes."*

(Pinocchio's nose grows longer)

*Wally DiCioccio, Jr.*

- "*Damn, with a nose like that you're never gonna get any action, Pinocchio.*"

- "*Don't worry, I know this blue fairy chick and someday she's gonna make me a real man!*"

My brother is a weird guy. When he was born I thought he was temporary. I thought he crawled to our front door, slipped my mom $20, and asked to stay the night. Two years passed and the kid was still there…playing with my toys. Then I began thinking that maybe he was like Alf, he crash landed here from another planet and now we're stuck with him. I remember one time he tried running away when my dad made him upset. He came home a few minutes later. So I told my mom to stop feeding him. Then she began dressing him just like me. Was one of me not good enough? Great, not only does he use my toys, but he shops at the same department store as I do. He might be my little brother but he's taller than me. One time we were playing catch in the fog, that's all I could see were his ankles. Sometimes when we'd fight I used to call him a son of a pup, but then I would quickly take it back because I would realize I was also insulting my mother.

Smokey the Bear is a great character too. The only problem with this guy is that he never had a nemesis. What's a hero without a villain? There should be an evil bear who just runs around the forest starting fires. This bear should be named, Clear Air The Bear, as opposed to Smokey. He won't let little girls eat his soup, or sit in his chairs. The guy doesn't have any chairs left to sit on, he burnt them all. Goldie Locks can't sleep in his bed either. He doesn't own one. This guy doesn't hibernate, he stays awake the whole time! Yes that's right, the whole entire time! He just runs around and around all year lighting stuff on fire. He tries making the forest as smoky as can be. His slogan could be, "Stop, Drop, and Roll a Joint".

Going to the zoo was always fun. All the animals just lounge around and sleep. I was so excited to go see the lion. He lived his life as the King of the Jungle, and now he's retired and lives with his family in the city. I would get so mad. I'd go see the lion and he'd just lounge around. Whooptie Doo! So I started yelling at him, *"Get up, do something!!"*. The lion sat up, looked at me and said,

- *"You want to see some action? Bring me that female zebra from pen 17. I'd like to take a bite of her!! I'm sick of steak everyday."*

Seals are funny looking animals. They really are. Humans must have discovered seals after discovering catfish, because there is no other possible reason why they just didn't go right ahead and call seals catfish. Roll them a ball of yarn, they realize they don't have any paws, so they bounce the damn thing on their noses. They're not afraid of swimming with killer whales. Why should they be? They have nine lives!

Wouldn't it be cool if humans had a mating season? I mean, every mammal has a mating season. Why not humans? We'd just be doing it left and right, here and there. Then when the season is over you'd look at each other like, "It got weird didn't it?".

## In the Classroom

When I was a kid, going to school was like torture. I used to pretend I was sick so my mom would let me stay home. I would just love sitting home and watching cartoons. Nickelodeon was the station to watch. I would hate when my dad came home from work because then I had to pretend I was twice as sick. After a while the old thermometer-to-the light bulb trick didn't work anymore. My mom would drag me to school by my ear and literally have to throw me into my classroom and luck the door. I remember my classmates were like, *"thermometer-to-the-light bulb trick didn't work on her today, huh?"*.

9

My bus driver was one scary dude. He looked like he never cut his fingernails in his life. They were lime green. The guy always had this serious poker face of death. He looked like he could have been a WWII vet. Every time we would get too rowdy these veins would pop out of his forehead. He never really yelled at us, but he seemed like he could have been a loose cannon at any second. His steering wheel was huge! It looked like a hula-hoop. We never wore our seatbelts because either your seat had two belts or two buckles. Never one belt and one buckle. My bus driver was always in a hurry. Why did he care? He didn't get detention if he came in late. I remember my friends would write obscene messages on the steamed up windows, but they soon realized the people outside couldn't read backwards.

In gym class we had two choices. You either shot hoops or climbed a giant yellow cargo net. I never climbed the net though. If I got up it, I'd probably be too afraid to come down. My favorite classes were Study Hall and Lunch. In Study Hall I would throw paper airplanes. In Lunch I would throw food. History class was nap time and Math class gave me serious brain damage. Science class was very exciting, we learned about rocks, and English class was cool because it sure beat taking French. Every time we had to write book reports I would rent the movie instead of actually reading the whole entire book. My teacher caught me once. Who knew Forrest Gump the book was so much different than Forrest Gump the movie?

I used to crush over these popular girls who never liked me because I was never popular enough for them. I hung out with a group of guys who would make fun of you for not having the balls to ask a girl out, yet they would also make fun of you if you did have the balls and got rejected. It was a lose-lose situation. I always wanted to be one of the cool guys at school. They could step in dog crap and still smell good. They were flawless. It's like they got a ticket to ride without even paying admission and I on the other hand missed the train by a mile…and I had a ticket.

I remember school dances in Junior High. All of the girls would stand on one side of the gym and all of the guys would stand on the other. I used to bring my binoculars just to check out all the chicks. Nobody danced. The whole school would have failed if we had to take a final exam in dancing. If I had danced with a girl in Junior High I would have probably went home believing she was my destined wife-to-be. It wasn't until High School when I watched Grease. I was amazed. I was like, *"Oooh, that's what we were supposed to do???!"*.

In Home Ec. class I learned how to make pillows and bake cookies. I'd be lying if I told you any of this has come in handy. I'm still yearning for the day to come when I have time to sew myself a pillow and bake a batch of cookies.

## It's a Mad World

Us humans are funny people. We'll drink potions that'll make us lose our perception and have us make bad decisions. We'll whip our partners for erotic pleasure. We'll create harmful drugs to inject into ourselves, and we spend millions of dollars on launching people into an atmosphere which we can't even breathe in.

I'm proud to say I'm not a smoker. There has to be something in cigarettes that makes you a little cuckoo upstairs. I think people who smoke are all a little crazy.

*Wally DiCioccio, Jr.*

- "Man, I'm tired of coughing. I have the worst cold. I can really go for a cigarette right now."
- "Dude, I'm so exhausted. It's so hot out! I can sure go for a smoke right about now."

I can just imagine these people on diets.

-"Whoa, this sucks! I gained 30 lbs in two months!! (clears throat)...Yes, I'd like to order a quarter pounder with cheese and four cups of lard please."

What do they do when they're cold? Sit their naked butts on a bucket of ice?

They think they're special too. They have a whole area reserved for them at restaurants. At my work the smokers get breaks whenever they want because if they don't get them they will supposedly "freak out". Smoking is like prolonging a suicide. Everybody is dying of cancer these days. If a guy gets stabbed seven times in the back the autopsy will probably say he died of cancer.

*Wally DiCioccio, Jr.*

Now we have all sorts of problems in this world and nobody has answers. Everyone is always searching for answers. We ask our friends for advice but they really don't know what to tell us. Nobody has the answers. Then in other rare circumstances people will have answers and they'll be searching for a problem. These people are nothing but troublemakers. I'm not just talking about women here either, I'm talking about algebra people. These people give you the answers then they make you solve the problem. First off, I'll tell you what the problem is, the problem is they already solved it for me. They gave me the answer. The problem is solved: $x + 5 = 10$, *find x*. Why should I solve the answer? They already told me the answer is 10. That's it, just 10, not 9, not 11, but 10. Well let's see, what adds to 5 that amounts to 10? Hmm, there is only one number that can do this...Ah Yes, 5 itself!! *5*

+ 5 = 10, I learned that way back in first grade. I'll tell you what the problem might be here. I think I figured it out. This 5 might be so ashamed of himself that he wanted to go in disguise. Maybe 5 wanted a makeover. Maybe 5 didn't like being a number waiting in the number line, 5 wanted to be a letter. One of the 26 letters of the alphabet. Maybe 5 was it's slave name and it would much rather be known as *x* now. There is your problem. The answer is still 10. Then they ask me to *find y*. Get the heck out of here, I just told you *y*!!!

Have you seen these television commercials selling phone books? I just use the phone book that my telephone company drops off at my doorstep. Who would go out of their way to buy a different brand?

- *"Man, I need that phone book! The one I have just isn't doing it for me."*

Could you even tell the difference? The phone numbers will most likely remain the same. They don't change from book to book. The only thing different is the cover.

Going to the dentist is always fun. You sit in a recliner and let a wealthy man stick his hands down your throat. I hate when he tells you to open your mouth wider. You can only open your mouth so wide. Its not like we're dogs or anything. Then as he is operating on you he always tries to strike up a little conversation. Who does this guy think he is, a hairdresser? I usually reply with, *"Uh huh"*, because you can't really say much else when your mouth is wide open and the guy is drilling your tooth. He asks me all of these personal questions. What, is he my shrink now?  If you ever really want to freak your dentist out, just stare right into his eyes the whole time he is operating on you.  If you want to piss your dentist off just eat a box of raisins before your appointment.  If you want him to leave the room for a few minutes so you can have time to spit, all you have to do is fart really loud.  It'll definitely catch him off guard.

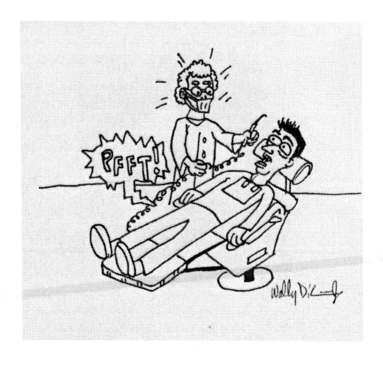

Have you ever kicked a mascot in the ass? Well, neither have I.

There is so much ridiculous paraphernalia in this world. The number one thing that comes to mind is the party hat. What is this? Do we *really* need these things? You put it on, you party. You take it off, party stops. Everybody goes home. Can we not throw a party without wearing a party hat? I was invited to this party once and I showed up without a party hat on my head. Imagine my embarrassment. I was the only person there not wearing one. In my opinion, I was the only person there who didn't look stupid. But everybody gave me the same puzzling look. I felt like I landed on another planet. They had this loud dance music playing. Everyone was standing around staring at me with these colorful cones on their heads. My buddy was actually embarrassed he invited me. He pretended he didn't know who I was or why I was even there. What gets me is somebody actually invented the party hat.

- *"Hmm. Let's see, I've got my scissors, some cheap cardboard, a broken rubber band, and a stapler. Maybe I should bend the cardboard into a cone. Ah yes, perfect! Then I can staple the rubber band to the bottom of it so people can strap this sucker to their heads without it falling off. I just might have to decorate this thing to make it more presentable to the public. It looks a little plain."*

Pirates are interesting individuals. They're ale guzzling voyagers of the ocean, in search of chests of gold, and if needed they'll battle anybody who stands in their way. I can just imagine these guys playing a game of Twister on their free time.

- *"Left hand, green."*

- *"Argh!!"*

- *"Right hook, yellow...Left peg, blue."*

- *"Ouch! Shiver-me-timbers Black Beard, you almost poked me good eye out with that thing!!"*

Twister...a land-lover's game

I hate the news. It's always bad news. The good news is always too ridiculous to even care about. Who cares if Big Bird is signing autographs at the local mall? By the way, is Big Bird a guy or a girl? After all, he does wear eye shadow. Anyway the news is always about some psycho killing their mom, or some place burning down. Then they show footage of people getting injected with drugs by syringes on the five o'clock news. I'm trying to eat dinner and these idiots are showing people in surgery and the dead bodies of Saddam Hussein's sons. The meteorologists are always so opinionated, *"It's going to be a very nice day tomorrow, sunshine and no rain!"*. Well, what if I wanted it to rain buddy? Not very nice for me now, is it?

Denny's is the place to be. I'm at Denny's all the time. If there were no such place as Denny's, I don't know where I'd go. When nobody can agree on anywhere else to eat, Denny's is the default place to go. It's a nice place to sit and talk. It's great because it's open all night. You get all sorts of crazy people coming and going throughout the night. Some people actually live at Denny's. I actually think the booths fold out into futons. I go back the next day, the same people are still sitting there, and the same servers are still serving. The coffee keeps flowing, the flapjacks keep flapping, and the weirdoes keep yapping.

They always have them claw machines at Denny's. You always see the girl come in with her tough boyfriend and suddenly nothing in life is more important to him than winning her a pink hippopotamus with the claw.

*- "Table for two?"*

*- "Not yet lady, hang on!! First I gotta get this damn thing. Then I can eat, and then I can sleep tonight. No punk is gonna leave here tonight with my girl's hippo!! I'd break their face! This little guy has got her name all over him!"*

27

*- "Um alright, just let me know when you're ready to be seated."*

The guy ends up blowing ten dollars in quarters. The damn claw doesn't even apply any pressure. It's an optical illusion. It can get pretty aggravating. It's tough because it's also timed. If you take too long the damn thing goes all by it's self. It's pretty harsh actually. For fifty cents there shouldn't be a time limit. At least give the person some time to think of a strategy. I mean, you put fifty cents in a jukebox and it plays a song for a good three to four minutes. You put fifty cents in a pay phone and you have a few minutes to talk as well.

The stuffed animals are always packed in there so tightly too.

*- "Maybe if I pull it by it's leg…"*

Have fun buddy, Magilla Gorilla is sitting on it's face!

In New York you're not allowed to smoke in bars or restaurants anymore, which I strongly support. I remember when it was legal though. Denny's was divided into two classes. You had the smokers and the non-smokers. The non-smokers sat in the diner and the smokers sat in a gigantic fish tank off to the side of the restaurant. They had their own little society in there. It was like their own little world with a polluted little atmosphere. They had fans in there that never worked. They made the fans at the same factory where they made the claw machine. They're made to look like they work, but they really don't.

Some meals at Denny's are named after baseball terminology. Last time I went I had the

Grand Slam. My buddy had a Few Walks and an RBI. Next time we go I'm getting a Perfect Game and he's going to order a Bunt with a side of hash browns.

I love the waitresses there too. They pour more coffee on your table than they do in your cup. They always ask you how everything is. They'll ask you at least seventeen times. They don't just ask you if the food is fine, they ask you how everything is. It's a very vague question. My mouth is always full, I can never answer properly. They should ask me when I pay the bill.

Has someone ever gotten really excited to tell you a funny story and by the end of it you don't even find it even a tad bit humorous? They tell you about something funny that happened between them and a person you never even heard of. Then you have to pretend you care.

"It was so funny!  My neighbor came out of her house licking a lollypop in her pajamas!"

Then they realize that you're not laughing so they throw you that world famous cover-up.

-"I guess you had to be there!".

-"Well you know, as a matter of fact I wasn't there!  You knew I wasn't there to begin with.  Why were you so excited to tell me this story if I can't even relate to it?  I don't even know who the hell you're talking about, so I can't even imagine this "funny event" taking place.  What, is she allergic to lollypops or something?  Does she have leopard print pajamas? Is she an older woman?  I'm sorry, but I don't get it dude."

31

*Wally DiCioccio, Jr.*

Last week I went to a parade.  It still amazes me how so many people are attracted to watching other people walk down a street to the beat of music.  While I was there, I saw a herd of them old Scottish dudes playing their bagpipes. You know, why don't they hand out earplugs as trinkets?  Why put us through the misery?  They should flash warning lights and post signs up to inform the crowd when the geezers in skirts are about to arrive.  Then we'd know exactly when to insert our earplugs.  I'm at the point where I don't even have to hear these guys.  I know what song they're going to play.  The damn tune is still ringing in my head from the last time they played it.  Even a person who went deaf knows which song they're playing.  You know, the one that sounds like an elephant on ecstasy walking in the middle of traffic?  There's never just one pack of these guys.  After the first pack left I was like,

"Thank God!", and not even two minutes later, once again without warning, an even larger pack arrived. Unlike the other guys, these guys are wearing red skirts. Different skirts, same damn song! I didn't know it at the time, but I guess the first pack of pipers were generics. This group supposedly sounded better because they had an additional nerdy kid walking behind them banging a big drum. I guess it's just not a parade without the bagpipers.

Have you ever sneezed and farted at the same exact time? It's an odd combination, *"Bless you"*, *"Thank you and excuse me"*. You've got snot running down your face, you've soiled your pants. It's not a good thing. I don't recommend it to anyone.

You know, it's easier than you think to make a fortune. Just look at a Q-Tip. Somebody came up with this wonderful idea. A little stick with cotton at the ends. Think of all the endless uses a Q-Tip can have. They actually have television commercials for cotton. One time I was just sitting in front of my TV and a cotton commercial came on, now I don't know what they did, but they sure convinced me. I got up and went to buy a bag of cotton balls. Cotton balls can come in handy. When I was a kid I was always getting ear infections. I was the silly looking kid in class with the wad of cotton stuck in his ear. It's easy to make a fortune though. You go to your local garden shop and you can buy such things as grass, dirt, and even rocks. Some guy actually sat there and wracked his brains out trying to think of what he could sell to make a profit. I bet all he did was look down and notice he was sitting on a rock.

-"*That's it!!! I can sell rocks to people who don't have any rocks! There has got to be somebody who needs rocks in this world.*"

The crazy guy was right. It was a desperate idea, but it actually worked. We use rocks to decorate our landscape.

My favorite one is the guy who thought of selling bagged air. I'm sure he thought it was an extremely stupid idea and laughed about it. Then when he realized people were actually interested in buying large amounts of bagged air, he laughed all the way to the bank. I guess they use it to pack boxes with instead of those little Styrofoam peanuts, which are a hazard to the O-Zone layer.

Then there is the most popular one, bottled water. This guy was probably first to come up with the idea of home plumbing and somebody ripped off his idea before he could even reveal it. I'm sure he felt bewildered, and thought to himself,

- *"Now what can I do to make a profit from something as simple and natural as water? Ah yes, I've got it!! I can bottle the water and tell people it's cleaner and healthier than tap water!"*

Now the guy is rolling in dough. For all you women out there reading this, don't think I'm sexist. I'm sure these things might have been thought of by women, but I just tend to say "guy". If there are five girls sitting in a room, I'd walk in and say, *"hey guys!"*. No matter where I go I see people with bottled water though. Even scuba divers have bottled water strapped to their belts! I don't know about you, but if beer were to flow from my kitchen sink, I'll be damned if I ever went out and spent money on a bottle of beer

37

ever again.    I don't care if it's supposedly healthier or not.


Have you ever insulted someone's mother and you later find out their mother is actually dead?  It's tough man, it's tough.


The other day I went to a thrift store to browse.  They sold used clothes, used TVs, used toys.  Wouldn't it be gross if they sold toilet paper at thrift stores?

I then went to purchase a chess set at a pawnshop but they didn't have any chess sets there.  Can you believe they *only* sold pawns??!  I never knew there was such a demand for pawns. I just ended up buying sixteen pawns, eight black, and eight white.  I had to go somewhere else for the board and the rest of the pieces.  After a little clash, I decided to put the kings in separate bags because the rest of the pieces made them feel insecure. They just kept yelling, *"Check! Check!"*.

*Wally DiCioccio, Jr.*

I figured a chess set would make a great conversation piece for my living room. Have you ever wondered what a conversation piece actually is? A conversation piece can pretty much be anything.

- *"Oh, this will make a great conversation piece!! I absolutely have to buy it!"*

You say that when you buy it, but will this day ever come? You have some company over and you're all sitting around and suddenly the whole conversation gets flat. Everyone in the room grows bored. You don't know what to do with yourselves. Then it hits you. You don't need to panic.

- *"Hey guys, check out this new chess set I bought. Its completely made of real crystal!! Let's talk about it. Albert, you go first."*

- *"Uh…well, both sides have an equal amount of bishops."*

- *"Good, thank you Albert. An equal amount of bishops, now isn't that something?! Okay Nancy, your turn!"*

I never win anything from lottery tickets. To me, nothing is more worthless than a lottery ticket. Not only do I waste money buying them, but I'm also ripping off the person I give them too as gifts. It's a lose-lose situation. It's also terrible when you give someone a lottery ticket and they end up winning big. You pretend to be happy for them but you're really kicking yourself in the butt. Purchasing a lottery ticket is like buying fresh air. Giving someone a lottery ticket can be very harsh.

-" *Happy Birthday Frank, I know you're already a loser, but here, scratch this ticket to confirm it.*"

-" *Happy Mothers Day Mom, here is a ticket to nowhere! Since you're not scrubbing the bathtub or the kitchen floor today, here, you can scrub away at this ticket!*"

-"*Happy 94th Birthday Uncle Jake, scratch this ticket and waste three minutes of your life.*"

For those of you who are addicted to gambling and never win, here is a good suggestion for you. Go up to a pop machine, buy a can of pop with a $5 bill, and wait for your change. CHA-CHING! - Believe me, it'll make you feel like you struck a jackpot! That machine will just be spewing out quarters for you to enjoy.

## You Gotta Have Faith

You know what the world's biggest mystery is? Religion. It really is.

The whole question of "why are we here?". I happen to be Catholic, but there are so many religions out there. I think it's basically all the same. I don't know what the big deal is. You stand up, sit down, stand up, sit down, kneel, pray, stand up again, sing a song, and shake hands. Can't we all just get along? I compare choosing religions with going to the movies. If I go to the movies with my friends and they want to see *Gandhi* and I want to see *The Ten Commandments*, I don't prepare for battle. We

45

eventually make up our minds and agree on something. If you're still not sure of which movie to see, just flip a coin or something. It's not that hard. If the movie is bad, oh well, you'll probably never watch it again. You'll live, life goes on. If you really cannot agree on one movie at all, then don't see a movie. Do something else instead. See, I don't go around and tell people what to believe. Why can't some people except other peoples' differences? I say believe what you want, if you happen to be wrong its not your fault. You were told it was the truth at one point or another.

Nobody knows how God looks. When I picture God I picture a bright cloud dubbed with the voice of Darth Vader saying things like,

(to his disciples)

- *"Mathew, Mark, John, and Luke, I am your father."*

(to Jesus)

- *"Impressive, young Skywalker."*

(Jesus to God)

- *"Skywalker? C'mon Pops, you can call me Landwalker, or heck, you can even call me Waterwalker, but **please** don't call me Skywalker!!! At least not until Easter for that matter."*

If Moses were alive today I'd picture him being a boxing referee.

(Ring Announcer)

- *"In this corner, from the Middle East, the Egyptian Stallion, The Red Sea. And in the other*

*Wally DiCioccio, Jr.*

corner, also from the Middle East, the other half of the Red Sea."

(throwing punches)

Moses: *"Okay, break it up...break it up!!"*

I can picture O.J. Simpson going to confession.

Priest: *"Okay, okay, hang on here.  So let me get this straight.  So you saw her with another man and you just happened to have a knife, gloves and a mask at hand?"*

O.J.: *"Well, I just happened to have a mask in my pocket.  When I was approaching them I stumbled across a knife and a pair of gloves.  So I figured, what the heck."*

*i'M SeRiOuS.*

Priest: *"Don't worry about it, go say five Hail Marys, and three Our Fathers and I'll-eluia later!"*

# The Sports Page

There are some crazy sports out there. Rugby is a crazy sport. Does this game have rules? Are these guys on drugs? There are so many guys on each team. Why don't they just join the army? Then they would fight over something more than a funky shaped ball. They just run around, pass the ball, kick the ball. Sometimes they can't make up their minds. Have you seen this ball? It looks like they got the instructions on how to make a basketball mixed up with the instructions on how to make a football. This thing is huge! These guys use wrestling moves to tackle players. No wonder the XFL went out of business.

I'm not a racecar fan either. That's all you do is drive in circles at approximately 187 mph with 42 other cars and see who passes the finish line first. I think 43 cars at a time is a bit crazy. They should only have three cars race at a time. There would be less accidents that way. The prize for winning a race is a huge check. I can just imagine Dale Earnhardt dragging these things into his bank.

*- "Howdy, I'd like to deposit 90% of this and cash the rest. Oh, and if it's not a problem, could you give me a receipt the size of a door please?"*

I remember when Dale Earnhardt drove himself to his death. Dale got in an accident on his final lap of the Daytona 500. Do you remember this? Everyone was so surprised, they called it a tragedy. NASCAR fans all around the world were sitting in sports bars mourning in awe like, *"This isn't supposed to happen! The guy was superhuman! He was a legend, a hero! What do you mean he died?!".* I don't think it was a tragedy. I wasn't shocked a bit. I wasn't surprised that "Mr. Racecar Driver" was in a racecar accident. I *would* have been surprised if he was mauled to death by a 730 lb ferocious tiger in the middle of the Amazon. Now that's a shocking tragedy! If you were a soldier in a war and died in a battle, that's not shocking to me. The odds are likely.

They made a big fuss about it too. He was on the cover of magazines, the front page of newspapers, television, candy bar rappers, boxes of Rice-A-Roni, canisters of Tang, packages of fish sticks, you name it. They made just as big of a fuss when JFK Jr. died in a plane crash, and he's a Kennedy! Earnhardt drove a racecar, but he's somehow just as famous. Thousands of children die every year in Africa of starvation and disease, but give Dale a giant cardboard check; he deserves it. After all, he drove in circles faster than the rest! If I drove in circles at 187 mph I'd get pulled over by a cop and have to pay a fine (well, if he could catch up to me). Where's my giant check? Why aren't companies asking me for endorsement deals?

Boxing is kind of like professional wrestling. Well, without the dropkicks, sleeper holds, and costumes. Okay, so it's nothing like professional wrestling. It's like a controlled bar fight. You just keep punching the guy until he falls over for at least ten seconds. Somewhere in this country there is a kid who is getting in fights at school all of the time. His principal tells him there is no future in fighting. The principle calls the kid's father and tells him about the fight. The kid goes home and his dad is on the phone with Don King, telling him the complete opposite.

Professional wrestling was the most interesting and fun thing to watch when I was younger. Yeah, I found out wrestling was fake last year so I stopped watching it. Hulk Hogan was the greatest. He still is, he was like a real-life Superman to me. I honestly think Hogan is the greatest wrestling legend ever. I'd wake up every Saturday morning to watch *The Three Stooges* and wrestling would air right afterwards. The matches had no competition, "Macho Man" Randy Savage would face some unknown guy named Leopold Harrison, and Bret "the Hitman" Hart would challenge the infamous Sammy Edwards III. I hate to use the word challenge because for Randy and Bret it wasn't a challenge at all. Wrestlemania was a special annual event that basically meant, "Who Wants to Get Beat By Hulk Hogan This Year?". I loved it when Hulk fought Andre "The Giant". Andre was a tall, out of shape fat guy with the fakest head-butt in history. He had no moves. Andre was the antonym of athletic. That was back when steel chairs were illegal objects. When Miss. Elizabeth was the only female in the ring. Back when refs pretended to do their jobs. Wrestling referees crack me up. They really do. They go back and forth and pretend they're keeping the match under control. Every time a wrestler nails his opponent, the referee grows this disgusted look on his face like, *"that's gotta hurt!"*. I used to collect all of the toys. I remember I even had a toy wrestling ring. It came with three ropes. Now they come with little chairs, ladders, barbed wire, brass knuckles, sand, an issue of Penthouse, and a pipe bomb.

Curling.  Now here's a *real* sport!  A group of Canadians slide heavy tea kettles across an ice rink and try to get them to stop on a target.  If the kettle slows down on it's way towards the target, a teammate grabs a broom and sweeps away at the ice hoping to make it more slipperier.  Sounds like hours of fun doesn't it?   Where do they purchase their sporting equipment, at the Home Depot?  After the games they all go out to the bar for some beer.  I say just skip right over the game and just go right for the beer instead.

Basketball is such a wimpy sport.  It really is.  It's almost just as bad as curling.  A guy bumps into you and you get two free throws.  It just seems ridiculous to me.  You knock a guy down and you get free throws.  I would just keep knocking guys down until they get fouled out of the game.  I really don't think players should be able to take shots from under the basket or from inside of the 3-point line. It should be 3-pointers or nothing. I'm serious, 2-point shots are so cheap. Where is the talent in that? It should be either one-on-one or two-on-two, like tennis. Now that is skill. Dunking should be illegal. You should get ejected from the game if you touch any part of the net with your hands. You don't belong that close to the basket. When Tiger Woods makes a putt, you don't see him pick the ball up and stick it right into the hole with his hands. That is something a little kid would do, not a professional athlete or a grown man for that matter. Personally, I see basketball like that game at the fair with the milk bottles. You know, the one where you have to stand behind a line or behind a counter and you have to knock all of the bottles off of the base by throwing a softball at them? They won't give you a stuffed animal if you cross the line. You don't see a bowler run up the alley and stuff the ball right into the pins. It's kind of like hunting deer. You don't walk right up to the deer and blow it's head off. You stand far in the distance and take your best shot at it. If you hit the deer and it runs away- oh well, give yourself credit, you tried. If you kill it- great job, three points! I tried out for basketball once and they told me I was too short. I came back the next day on stilts. They told me I was too white and I didn't have game. I returned the third day painted black, on stilts with a box of Monopoly. The coach didn't know what to say. He asked me if I knew how to dribble. I said, *"Are you kidding? I knew how to drool since the day I was born!"*. The coach got mad and told me to leave. Then he called me a smart ass. Seriously, I took it as a compliment. Most asses are dumb.

Jockeys are weird looking guys. They all look the same. They're taller than midgets, but shorter than the average man. They sound like they've been sucking helium all day. Where do these guys come from? Is there an island set off somewhere where jockeys are born? You don't see jockeys anywhere else. They're always riding horses. You'll never see a jockey flipping burgers, giving an oil change, or working behind a desk. Is this genetic? If you're born a jockey, do you grow up to be a jockey? It's like communism or something. Maybe the horse breeders breed jockeys too. Most three year olds learn how to ride tricycles, these kids are being trained how to ride ponies. It must be tough growing up as a jockey in school. All of the kids must make fun of your flashy patterned sweaters and your matching helmets. Horseracing is a unique sport. There are animals involved. Your teammate is a horse. It's like the jockey is the coach and the horse is the athlete. The teamwork strategy is inhumane though. The jockey just beats the horse's ass in order to get it to run faster. I would dress myself and the horse in some armor and unleash a cheetah on the track. Then I'd see how fast my horse would run. You don't see horse helping guys out in any other sport. You don't see guys stealing second base on horseback when you're watching baseball. Although you do see father and son duos assaulting first base coaches.

Although I love watching football, baseball is my favorite sport. I'm a big Yankee fan. I'm not sure if I'd be a Yankee fan if my dad hadn't injected the Yankees into my blood at a very young age. My friends were fans of Nolan Ryan and Jose Canseco, but I would tell them I liked Maris and Mantle. They wouldn't even know who the heck I was talking about. My bedroom looks like a small sector of the National Baseball Hall of Fame. I remember when the Yankees beat the Mets in the World Series. My dad popped a bottle of champagne down our stairwell and got it all over my mom's new carpet.  He spent hours licking it up.

You know, I've been watching baseball for years and not once have I actually seen a bull warm up in the bullpen.  I love the umpires too. Whenever you need a ball, just ask the ump.  The guy is like a ball machine!  The catcher extends his arm out and within seconds the ump places a new ball in his hand.  It's like magic!  I love hecklers.  A baseball game just isn't a baseball game without hecklers.

- *"Hey Rodriguez, you're a bum!!  You smell like crap, Rodriguez!!!  My grandma can hit better than you, Rodriguez!!  Can't you hear me??!!  What, you want me to speak Spanish??!!!?"*

## On With the Show

I love going to the movies. You can watch someone's life story in two hours time. Movies are fantastic. They can make you laugh, they can make you cry. Heck, they can even make you scream until you soil yourself.

I love how movie heroes can get shot at 7,896 times and only have a paper cut on their cheek. It's amazing! In horror movies the killer is always someone you least expect. Just once I want to see the guy who was named a suspect in the first ten minutes of the film end up being the killer. Everyone will feel like fools afterwards.

- *"It was him all along?!??   And we wracked our brains out this whole time for nothing??!!"*

Musicals crack me up.  Everything is all dramatic and all of a sudden everyone starts singing about what's going on at that very moment.  Suddenly everybody in town cares about the same thing.  They care enough to all join together and sing about it joyfully.  Somehow they all know the lyrics on cue.  They should have a horror movie musical.

*(Broadway music playing)*

- *"Gash!  I'll stab her in the neck again.  Slash! I'll cut her into coleslaw, and then…Die!  I'll slay her with my chainsaw, my friend, and hide her in a pond!!"*

The whole "going to the movies" experience is fun in itself, really. There are always the thirteen years old punks sitting in the front row laughing like hyenas, the make-out lovebirds, the fifteen year old slackers throwing popcorn at people and pointing to the characters' private parts with laser-pointers, the retired couple that look like they'd be more entertained if they were watching water boil, and the black women yapping on their cell phones and predicting what's going to happen next.

Pee Wee's Playhouse was a great show to watch when I was a kid. Pee Wee was the man. He had a couch that talked, a cow for a neighbor, flowers that sang, a TV that you can jump into and connect dots, a gay genie, a cowboy, a hooker, a trash talking marionette, a robot, miniature dinosaurs that lived in mice holes, a talking floor, an 8 foot tall ball of foil, a flying

Pterodactyl, a talking globe, a jazz band of puppets, a sailor, a postal worker, and two chuckling fish. Kind of reminds me of Michael Jackson's ranch.

Everybody is going crazy for these reality TV shows lately. This *American Idol* show is really starting a frenzy. Since when has anyone been this excited to watch a talent show? The show is called, *American Idol*, but it's only based on singing and vocals. Since when do idols have to have a great singing voice? Can't an idol be an entertainer, an athlete, a family member, or a politician? The show should be called, "Who Sings the Best?".

I don't listen to the radio anymore either. For every three songs they play, they play forty minutes of commercials. They're the same three songs that play all day long too. They drill the songs into your head until you buy the albums.

Don't you just love it when you buy the whole album and that one single song is the only song worth listening to on the whole entire CD? It drives me nuts. I hate when they have the news on the radio. I just want to hear some good beats when I drive. India and Pakistan are never going to make peace, just play some Red Hot Chili Peppers already.

## There Goes the Neighborhood

My house lies beside the home of the nosiest people on earth. My neighbors are a riot. They really are. Their favorite thing to do is protect our house. They sit in their windows and spy on us. They keep their eyes peeled for any irregular activity taking place in the neighborhood. They're good! Who needs a security system when you have them?

- *"Last night at 11:48 a red Mercury pulled into your driveway. There were two women inside the vehicle. They seemed suspicious. The one looked familiar, but I think she lost some weight since the last*

71

time we've seen her. The other woman was slightly older. We heard her mention something about going to the movies. The one was very outgoing. She's possibly a Libra. So, anyway, were they over to visit? Are they family or friends? What did they want? Were they selling Tupperware? We need some new bowls! Did they say they liked our new lawn ornaments? The flamingos were getting old."

# The Holiday Season

I never understood Halloween. You have your kids go house to house dressed like a character to collect candy from complete strangers. Gut a pumpkin, carve a face in it, and then when you're all finished place a candle inside and light it. It was fun though. The thing is, when you're a kid everything is big, magical, and extra special. When you're a kid simple things amuse you. When you're an adult they annoy you. I remember I used to get really excited every time my mom took me to the McDonalds drive-thru. It seemed like a magic trick to me. You pull the car up to the side of the building and people hand you bags of food with free little toys inside. Trick or Treat. What does this mean? I always got treats. Nobody ever tricked me before. Well, not on Halloween at least.

- *"Here have some candy!"*

(holds their hand out)

- *"Ha, I tricked you!! It's dog crap!"*

Christmas is my most favorite time of the year. Besides the crazy shopping season and all of the hustle and bustle, it still is my favorite time of year. You shop til' you drop, hang with the family, eat, eat, eat. Open presents, exchange presents, and did I mention eat? When I was a kid, I loved hearing about Santa. But the second I got on his lap I'd crap my pants. I'm serious, I don't know why, but I was afraid of him up close. So it was kind of ironic that he'd come when I was asleep. He seemed cool for an old guy. Unlike the rest of the company he would just come and go. He wouldn't linger around, eat all of the nuts and fall asleep on our couch like the other old dudes. Plus, he brought us presents for the simple price of some milk and cookies. Not one or two presents, a lot of them. I never wondered how he fit down the chimney either. He had the magic touch I guess. It was believable that he flew across the whole world in one night too because to me the whole world was my neighborhood. I didn't know anything about the world. I saw airplanes in the sky, but I thought they'd land at the end of my street and pick me up if I needed a lift to my friends house. Maybe that's why flying reindeer didn't phase me as being weird. I used to read comic books and idolize super heroes all day. Zorro was one of them heroes that never really appealed to me. He didn't have any super powers. Zorro didn't seem tough enough. He wasn't all he was "cut out" to be, no pun intended. Instead of killing the bad guys, he just gave them his initial autograph on their chests. I can picture a little Spanish guy walking up to Zorro and asking him to sign his dying son's chest.

- *"Hey Chico, my son is dying in the hospital of a rare disease, would you please sign his chest for him? He is a big fan. It'll just take a few seconds. Here, you can use my extra-fine tip Sharpie."*

- *"Sure, but what will I get out of it?"*

- *"I'll treat you out for some Taco Bell."*

*- "Okay, you have yourself a deal."*

You know, I think Santa Claus should have an enemy. Scrooge and The Grinch came close, but they ended up turning nice in the end. I'm talking about a bad guy, someone so incredibly cruel. A *really* scary guy. We'll call him Borox Claws. Instead of wearing a red suit, his is royal blue. Borox's beard isn't white, it's black. Pointy and black. His sleigh is pulled by 8 ferocious flying crocodiles. Borox doesn't come down chimneys, he breaks into your house through your front door. With a credit card. A maxed out credit card. Yeah, this guy is bad! He really is. He brings kids charcoal. Even when they're good. This guy isn't fat like Santa, he's skinny. His wife doesn't bake him cookies, serves him vegetables. He doesn't have elves working at his factory, he just has a shovel and a boxcar full of coal. He doesn't say, "Ho Ho Ho!!". He says, "Ahhuhu Huhua Hahaha!!".

With my family, the holidays revolve around food if you haven't noticed. When it comes to eating with Italian people the food is either one of two things. gewd-uh, or not-so-gewd-uh. There's gewd-uh bread, gewd-uh cookies, gewd-uh sauce, gewd-uh wine. Everything else is not-so-gewd-uh. Also, the bigger the size of the food, the better it is. There's always, "a-big-uh-leg-uh-lamb", "zucchini-like-a-deese", and "angel hair pasta". Tell them you grew a pepper that is a foot long and their eyes will light up.

You would think Easter would be a sad holiday where Catholic people morn Jesus's death. You would think we'd be wearing black and bringing roses to church, but everybody wears white and paints hard-boiled chicken eggs with dye. Then this magical giant rabbit comes to your house when you're asleep to bring you baskets of more colored eggs and chocolate. See, Santa has a sleigh and flying reindeer, this little dude has no vehicle either. The Easter Bunny goes solo. He's a loaner, a rebel. He hops all across the world in one night. Yet, the sorry guy couldn't even beat a turtle in the run-a-thon last month. Maybe all that hopping from house to house got to him. Poor guy.

## On the Job

Work is great isn't it? I love going to work. Why would I want to sit around and relax all day when I can go to work? Something weird happens on my way to work each day. Time jumps fifteen minutes into the future within only five minutes time. I can't figure it out. I think I must drive through these intergalactic wormholes or something. I get to work on time or a few minutes early and the punch-clock says I'm fifteen minutes late. You would think by now I would get the hang of it and go to work fifteen minutes early to be on time. Have you ever been at work and you just stop for a second and wonder what the heck you're doing there? At work I have to put on my Mr. Rogers face, smile as much as possible, and invite my customers back.

   - *"Hi, Good Afternoon! How are you doing? Fantastic! It's a beautiful day isn't it? Alrighty, have a good one, hope to see you soon!"*

My customers always look at me like I'm crazy. They look like they just got back from a funeral. Some of them are grouchy. We all can relate to this right? Sometimes you're the one behind the counter, sometimes you're the grouch. When you're behind the counter you don't like the grouch, when your the grouch you don't like the employee. Some people just enjoy being grouchy. They're always grouchy. They don't know how to act any other way. They think I know exactly what they want without them even telling me.   Like I can read their minds or something.

- *"Do you want to put this on your credit card Mrs. Anderson?"*

- *"Hell no, are you stupid?!!   If I charge one more item on my card the damn thing is gonna bounce, you dimwit!"*

My old boss was something else too.  She made the Wicked Witch of the West look like Shirley Temple.  You could smell the Alpo on her breath.  Its a good thing she wore high heels because you could hear her getting closer.  It would give you enough time to get the heck out of there.  Man, she was something.  If I would've thrown her into a shark tank the sharks would've thrown her back.  I still don't know why she was always pissed off.  Maybe she asked Satan on a date and he turned her down.  You know when you were a kid and your mother would tell you not to be afraid of old ladies and that they don't bite? I seriously believe my old boss would bite you if you got her mad enough. She was like a drill sergeant. Anytime she would order me to do something I would jump to it. It was do or die. She would light my ass on fire so I would move faster. She was always right about everything too. I could never question her judgment. If she was ever wrong I wouldn't dare tell her, I would just tell her she was absolutely right. It made the day move more smoothly. My new manager is very different than my old boss, but she still gets me to do things for her in a jiffy. She doesn't need to set my ass on fire though. The reason I do whatever she says is because she's hot. It's not fair. I'll never have an advantage.

I love it when I'm standing at work all day with my thumb up my butt and at the end of the day I get eleven last-minute shoppers just as I'm about to close down the register and lock the doors. Do they do it for spite? Do they not have any consideration? Do they think you can only purchase things at the end of the night just as I'm about to close? Maybe they think it's a contest to see how much stuff they can buy in the nick-of-time before the place closes. They're probably trying to set a new world record.

I once worked at a donut shop. I used to be a cashier at the drive-thru window. A lot of people never knew we were able to hear everything they were saying once their car pulled up to the spot where they ordered from. One time this guy was talking to somebody on his cell phone and I overheard him telling the guy he had just killed someone. The next thing I knew he had already pulled ahead to the pick-up window and he had blood splattered all over his face. In his passenger seat sat a plastic snowman. You know those light-up ones that people put on their front porches during the Christmas season? Well this guy had one in his car. It was wearing a seatbelt and everything. At first I didn't know what to think. He ordered a large black coffee, and then he asked me for another one for his snowman. I thought he was joking, so I asked him, *"Wouldn't coffee melt his organs??"*. He then stopped and changed his mind. He then ordered an iced cappuccino instead, so I asked him, *"Wouldn't that be kind of like cannibalism??!!"*. He didn't find it a tad bit funny. The guy then gave me the look of death and pulled my collar towards his snarling self. I thought I was going to die. In the most polite fashion, he simply asked me if I could be more kind to his snowman and treat it with some respect. I agreed, handed him his drinks, and I ran to the restroom like a wimp. Let's just say I'm not in the donut business anymore. The same weirdoes would come back three times a day for refills on their coffee. I don't know what the hell we put in that coffee, but it seemed like more than just caffeine.

## On the Road

I love driving to work. The drive to work is one of the most exciting obstacles of my day. My car is great. My car is *the man*. When I'm in my car it's like a whole other world. When I'm out of my car I'm a very patient guy, but once I'm in my car I'm always in a rush. Nothing stands in my way. There's a train crossing, no problem; I'll take the detour. Then there's an old lady driving a Rambler in front of me and all I can see are her hands on her wheel. Beat it lady, take a hike! You're on my turf now, Grandma! Where did she get her license, in a Cracker Jack box? I blast past her and give her a new hair-do. Then I race past a semi truck. The guy driving thinks he's all big and buff. Too bad he's only driving half of a truck and I'm speeding past him in my whole car. I don't stop for nobody, whether its a deer, an opossum, a woodchuck, a turkey, or even Bob Saget himself. There's no stopping me. You know the rules, yellow means hurry up, green means accelerate, and red means *"Damn It!"*. I can't stand sitting at red lights and seeing the people who have green lights moving. They're all accelerating happily. If I could fly, I would, and if I could I would hope I knew how to land. It's fun looking at the people in the cars next to you when you're at a red light. You wonder what they're thinking when they look at you. You give them that bitter look like, *"What are you looking at, punk?!"*. You never want them to see you when you're looking at them. You can hear what song is playing on their radio, so you roll your window down and play the song you're listening to louder. Yeah, that'll show them what's up.

## On the Web

Everybody is on the internet these days. Nobody leaves the house. We can go to work from our homes online. Next thing you know people will be going on cyber vacations. You won't even have to pack or worry about hotels or airfares. Pretty soon people will be getting married online. People who never even met in person. The priest, judge, or rabbi will just send you instant messages.

- *"Do you Bernard Michael Wilson take this woman to be your cyber wife?"*

*Wally DiCioccio, Jr.*

    - *"I do."*


I met a girl online once and we finally tried meeting in person. She looked nothing like she did in the picture she sent me.


    - *"Hi, are you Wally?"*


    - *"Yeah, who are you?"*


    - *"I'm Sarah, silly."*


    - *"No you're not, Sarah is half your size!"*


Let's just say that didn't go over too well.

I hate the junk mail I get online. Advertisements asking me if I would like to enlarge my penis. No thank you, I'm doing just fine without a third leg. I hate those chain letters I get too. At the end of the letter it tells you to forward the letter to every single person you have on your mailing list or else you'll get attacked by a wild bunch of baboons and be forced to watch Lord of the Rings ten times in a row. The Lord of the Rings was like The Wizard of Oz, but it just focused on the wizard and the munchkins. Instead of flying blue monkeys they had dog-faced warlords on horseback. These damn things chase this kid the whole movie because they want his magic ring. When the kid puts the ring on he disappears, but for some reason he takes it off. Now I don't know about you, but if I didn't want to be found I'd leave the damn thing on. Man, I couldn't even watch that damn movie from beginning to end as it is. I had to leave the theater before I fell asleep. Don't you love how the internet bombards you with pop-up ads? As if we don't see enough commercials on TV or in magazines. Buy Now, Order Now, Call Now, Save Now, Enter to Win Now. It's like a damn circus. Then they have the freak show section,

"Click Here to see Rosie O'Donnell naked!!". My God, I'd rather watch Lord of the Rings! The internet is full of polls too. They always want us rating things, "Who is Hotter, Britney Spears or Christina Aguilera?". Who really cares? Are they going to send the results to Britney or Christina? Like they need another reason to boost up their self-esteem. What's with all of these female rock bands out lately? Either you're Alanis Morissette or Green Day. Don't mix the two worlds. They look like drunk wannabees at karaoke night.

# The Queen City

I was born and raised in Buffalo, New York, otherwise known as, "The Home of Losers". When I was a kid I used to think the Super Bowl was an annual event to watch different teams beat the crap out of the Buffalo Bills. I wasn't even aware we had a hockey team until the Sabres managed to make it to the Stanley Cup. Buffalo is a weird place. On Halloween, kids go trick-or-treating on snowmobiles. Besides shoveling snow, there isn't really much to do around here. If you've never been here, you're not missing a thing. If you're interested in seeing tons of water rushing down the side of a cliff, you can find that at Niagara Falls, which is just a hop, skip, and a jump away from Buffalo. If you don't mind spending an hour digging your car out of a couple feet of snow every morning before work, driving to work in blizzards, or wearing a scarf on Independence Day, Buffalo is the place for you. Besides all of the chicken wing eating, there isn't much else going on in Buffalo. It's a ghost town. In downtown, Buffalo there is this huge monumental tombstone that reads: *"Here Lies Buffalo, New York."* Somebody once told me that Buffalo used to be a party city. It was the center of the Pan-American Exposition. Did you know that in 1901 Buffalo was like a Las Vegas of it's time? I'm serious, it was full of bright lights and glitz and glamour. Knowing this doesn't help much though. I don't care how great the city used to be, it's not that great anymore. Most of the big industries that were rolling in dough are now six feet under. Everyone around here calls

Buffalo, "downtown". They're absolutely right, it seems everything in town has gone, or is on the verge of going down. They call Buffalo, "the Queen City". That's just fantastic, we're New York's bitch. You have a better chance of seeing a blue moon here than you are of seeing the sun. The other day the weatherman mentioned the sun coming out and at first I thought he was talking about a groundhog or something. For a second there I forgot what the heck the sun was. That shows you how often I see the sun. Man, my skin is so white I make Casper look like a Mexican. Last summer I went to a local beach and when I got out of the water I was wearing a fishing net and a grass skirt made of seaweed. I took my sunglasses off so I could enjoy the sun for at least a few seconds and a seagull crapped right in my eye. What are the odds? The surface of most beaches consists of mostly sand. The surface of Buffalo beaches consists of dead fish and scattered trash. Us Buffalo people have our own ways of pronouncing words. We call soda "pop". If you don't like it then that's just too bad. The proper name for it is, "soda pop", but we're too lazy to say the "soda" part. You guys on the other hand are too lazy to say the "pop" part. If you're eating a garden salad you don't say you're eating a garden. You simply say you're eating salad. Get it? Got it? Good.

As I said, in Buffalo we get tons of snow each and every year. It snows for hours on end and then once it finally stops there is 3 feet of snow covering the ground, so I decide to bundle up, go outside, and shovel the driveway. Every single time I finish shoveling the snowplow guy finally decides to come down my street and plow the snow from the street back onto my driveway. Just when I think I'm done, I have a whole other task to do. I get this dark feeling in my stomach.

You can hear him coming from the end of the street. The yellow flashy lights get closer and closer. You can feel the ground rumble under your feet. I feel him approaching but it disgusts me to look. I hate the look the snowplow guy gives me. I glare at him, he looks over at me laughing. He knows what's up. He's enjoying himself. The guy looks 30 year old man who still thinks he's playing nose-tackle for the high school football team. He has a can of beer in one hand and the other on the steering wheel. This guy is having a great time, he's plowing snow, and pissing people off. An hour and a half later I go in the house, crack my back into place, and have a cup of coffee.

Have you ever wondered what the point of building snowmen was? Why do children build these things? They can make snowmonkeys, snowgiraffes, snowpyramids, or even snowwomen, but they all choose to sculpt fat men out of snow. Are they like scarecrow of the winter? Are they supposed to protect our homes? They're always smiling, they can't be too intimidating. They're always holding brooms too. I'm in my driveway shoveling my butt off and this guy is just standing over there on my front lawn watching me, holding a broom, not helping. What good is a broom? No wonder he's not helping me out, them damn kids made him all wrong. He was supposed to be holding a shovel. Either way, he'd still just be standing there holding a shovel. But the thing is, this guy is made completely out of snow. I don't think he would really enjoy shoveling snow. That's like us shoveling up guts and body parts. Maybe that's why the kids gave him a broom instead. These guys all look the same. They have their carrot noses, branch arms, no legs, scarf, gloves, and top hat. You never see a snowman with a potato for a nose, or a banana. No Jewish snowmen I guess. Snowmen are weird though. They look like mannequins displaying apparel for a thrift store.

*"Hey Steve, Thanks for coming. This is my house, there is my new car, and over there is my snowman, Mr. Shivers. He'd make a great worker if he could really sweep!"*

*Wally DiCioccio, Jr.*

## On the Sixth Day...

I'm sad to admit this, but I too am a man. Definitely not a snowman, but I'm a man nonetheless. Us men are socially retarded, We seriously are. Guys ask other guys simple questions. We don't answer the question, we just repeat it back to them.

- *"Hey, how are you?"*

-*" Oh Hey Wally, how you doin'?"*

It's like, *"Dude, I asked you first!"*

No matter how old or how wise we get, us guys will always find farting funny. There is just something about flatulent that tickles our funny bones.

Shaking hands is a strange ritual we all do. Personally, I don't prefer it. I only do it because it's how people greet each other. What's wrong with saying, "Hi", or just waving? I'll even give you a salute instead. Shaking hands just isn't my cup of tea, but as a person I have to do it. You extend your arm out and drop it down as if your hand is cutting through an imaginary head of lettuce. Sometimes its a quick shake, other times a drawn out shake. Sometimes they don't know when to stop. Have you ever met a guy who just loves shaking hands? He shakes your hand when you walk into the room, he shakes your hand when you leave. He pats you on the back, he's just constantly giving handshakes. Often you'll find the people who do the quick and formal shake, just so you know their being polite. Then there are the city boys who have the twelve-step handshakes that take weeks to memorize. It's like dance moves for hands. You snap your fingers and point your hand in the shape of a pistol. You give each other a five behind your back. Some guys have this shake like they're mixing a batter, like they're cranking a jack-in-the-box or something. Sometimes you'll clasp their hand

*Wally DiCioccio, Jr.*

while attempting to shake and your buddy will pull you towards him to bump shoulders together. Let me just say, my shoulder wouldn't be complete without coming in contact with another man's shoulder. Now I can sleep at night. Have you ever met a guy who has such a firm shake that he thinks he has to squeeze the blood out of your hand? It's like they're trying to warn you not to mess with them.

- *"You better watch out man, I'll squeeze your hand so hard you'll turn purple!!"*

# Daddy-O

My dad is a pretty interesting guy. He's the kind of guy that'll definitely squeeze your hand until you turn purple. My dad is pretty tough for a short guy. His vocabulary is pretty short too, it only consists of about 250 words. Actually, I should say 50, since he has 200 different meanings for the word "thing". He's quite the handyman. He owns a hammer, a wrench, and a bunch of "things" in a box. He breaks objects instead of fixing them. He always asked my brother Mike and I to help him.

-*"Go get the thing. I need it to fix this thing."*

-"*Where is it Dad?*"

-"*I think it's in the basement under the stairs, in that blue thing with a handle.*"

His excuse was, "*They don't make them like they used to.*" I disagree. He broke the door hinge in '93, and he breaks hinges now. Nothing has changed. They still make them like they used to. In his own world, he believes he's always right, slick, suave, fast, funny, tough, energetic, and handsome. When something has to be done, he does it. If something doesn't go his way, he asks God why everybody in this world is mental. If there is something on the floor and I walked passed it without picking it up, he would say,

"*Why didn't you pick that thing up? Can't you see it there? You know that thing don't belong there! What, are your eyes on your feet son?*"

112

I would simply say,

*"No, but if they were on my feet, I'd definitely see the thing on the floor Dad."*

Yeah, this is the guy I'm named after. He's a riot, he would watch "Who Wants to be a Millionaire" every single night. He thought there was a secret life-line where the contestant could hear him screaming the answers through our television set. If they got the question wrong, he would call them jerks.

He also loved watching "Wheel of Fortune". His favorite category was "THING". We have 500 channels including HBO, and he ends up watching a lady sell a latch-hook set on QVC.

You should hear him sing. He sings the lyrics, "Say ya would if ya could" to the tune of any song. He knows the name of the Prime Minister of Beijing, but he can't memorize the lyrics to Jingle Bells.

There are six rules that you must abide by that you should be aware of before eating dinner with him at my house.

1.) Do Not leave any food on your plate.
2.) Do Not say anything unless it is a true fact.
3.) Laugh only if he tells a joke.
4.) Roll up your sleeves if you're wearing a long sleeved shirt.

5.) Be prepared to take part in a history lesson and

6.) DO NOT leave any food in your plate!!!

He would always threaten to shove my uneaten food down my pants.

- *"What's wrong with them beans?"*

-*"Nothing, I'm full."*

-*" Eat them beans or else I'll shove them down your pants!!"*

My mom asked him if he liked her meatloaf, he replied,

-*"Oh it was pretty good, but Mickey Mantle was better."*

We didn't get along.   I liked Mickey Mouse, he liked Mickey Mantle.  He liked Elvis

115

and The Monkees, I liked Alvin & The Chipmunks. I liked the Beastie Boys, he liked the Beach Boys.

When I was younger I used to tell my buddies, *"I bet my dad can beat up your dad!"*. Then when my dad pissed me off it was more like, *"I'll pay your dad to beat up my dad!"*

Sure, he loves to order people around, but the guy don't even know how to order a pizza. My dad doesn't even know what to do when a phone rings. He yells at it and tells people to leave him alone. If you ring the doorbell, he'll answer the door and tell you he's not home. We have a cordless phone, and if by any chance he uses it, he still stands a cord's length from the wall.

If my dad ever asks you to go on vacation, just hide! Get the heck out of there like the is no tomorrow! Even if he brings a map he'll get lost. Several times. One time he took my family to

Cooperstown to see the National Baseball Hall of Fame. We stayed at a hotel that was built on a hill and tilted at a slant. I remember there was a picture hanging in the hallway of the Leaning Tower of Pisa. It was the first time I've seen it stand straight. I rolled out of bed 17 times that night. The shower sprinkled out brown sludge, and the soap was the size of my fingernail. When we needed room service, my dad just rolled downstairs and found somebody.

My dad loves to receive mail. He paces the entire house every single morning impatiently waiting for the mailman to come by. Then he'll put the news on at fifteen minutes after the hour. Why? Because that is exactly when the weatherman is on. My dad won't leave the house until he knows what the weather is going to be like first. He goes on and on about how happy he would be if the mailman would arrive, but when he finally does he usually hands my dad a few bills and troubled forms that got messed up somehow in the mail, forms that were never sent to their proper destinations. Then my dad starts yelling to an invisible army and tells them how much he hates the mailman and how the mailman never does anything right. He tells them that he can't depend on other people to do anything. Besides all of that, my dad is a great guy. He's one in a million.

## From Venus

We might seem pretty odd, but men aren't the craziest of the two sexes though. Guys, just go on a date and you'll find out for yourself. I took my last girlfriend out to eat and she thought her toothpick was an eating utensil. Here I had already eaten a steak and she only had three peas. Then she went to the restroom to cough them up. She was one crazy chick! She would buy half of the produce section just so she could apply the food to her face before bed. The first stages of dating are always a delight aren't they?

- *"You're a Virgo and your favorite color is blue too?!! No Way!! Weird, we are so alike! This is crazy, oh my God!!"*

Women are definitely from Venus, they make it seem like they're interested in smooth guys, but they're actually into the nerdy guys a lot more. They're just afraid of what their friends would think of him, so they find guys who their friends will approve of. Then they're shocked when they find their best friend in bed with their boyfriend.

Then there are the women who are more attracted to dead presidents than their lovers. They always want to know where I work, how much I make, and what kind of car I drive.

- *"Wanna go out for some coffee?"*

- *"I don't know, maybe. You look familiar, where do you work?"*

- *"Al's Donut Hut."*

- *"Oh really?  Well, do you drive a Mustang?"*

- *"No, an Escort."*

- *"Oh, well I'm not a coffee drinker, sorry."*

They don't even care what the guy is like. He just has to have a nice car and a lot of cash.

- *"I'm engaged to a doctor, he drives a Ferrari! Have you seen it?"*

- *"No, have **you** seen **him**?!  The guy looks like he works for the circus!!"*

All they see is green.  I think they forget to put them little glasses on when they go tanning or something.  By the way, I think women look hot

121

when they're tan, but sometimes enough is enough.

*- "Dave, this is my girlfriend Amy, she's orange. Isn't she so cute? She's my little tangerine."*

Girls tell me they don't like me because I'm too nice. Where the heck am I, in the Twilight Zone?! You would think being nice was a good thing. I think girls want a guy with 'edge'. Whatever the heck 'edge' is, I don't have any. I wouldn't consider myself Greg Brady, but on the other hand, I'm no Vin Diesel. Women want a tall guy with muscles who has nothing on his mind besides sports and tools. A guy who wears expensive clothes, drives an expensive car with an expensive stereo system in it. A guy who looks like he can beat the living crap out of anybody who stands in his way. A guy with nice teeth, fancy hair, a pretty face, and its a bonus if the guy walks like he's carrying luggage. Ladies want a man who knows his car parts more than he knows his own family. Then the guy can fix their car for the price of some quick sex. I honestly think I'm single because I don't know jack about cars, I just eat little ones made of chocolate.

With women everything is, *"Me, Me, Me!!"*. It's all about, *"Me"*. They want and want…and want.

- *"Listen to me, how do I look? Look at me! You're not even looking at me! What do you want from me? Don't you care about me? Did you hear what I said?! All you care about is sports!!"*

- *"Oh yeah? Well, all you care about is* **you!!!"**

Women love options. They love variety. They have to get the next best thing. Whether its flashy colors, items that shine, things that glow, stuff that smells nice, or just about anything that sparkles, girls will want it. Out with the old, in with the new. Women are obsessed with lotion. They're always lubing their palms up with this stuff and their hands are already baby soft to begin with. I don't get it. I guess they have nothing better to do.

I never knew this until just recently, but girls plan on what they're going to wear weeks in advance. I just wake up, open my closet, pick something to wear and put it on. Girls buy clothes to wear in advance. They have outfits in their closets that they've never worn before. They save them to wear for when the perfect time comes along. Sometimes the perfect time never comes. Sometimes the perfect time comes but they waited so long that they don't fit into them anymore. Sometimes they'll only wear something once and never wear it ever again. This applies to dresses, jeans, shirts, pants, jewelry, and shoes. Don't even get me started with women and shoes. They're addicted to shoes. They never have enough shoes. I wear the same pair for two years straight and in that same time period, girls will wear seventy different pairs.

A lot of women have cell phones these days. Now instead of calling them at home I can call their purses. The reason girls have these things is to block unwanted calls. Every time I call I end up leaving their purse a message because once they see it's me who is calling they don't bother answering. They don't even call me back for that matter. I try to imagine they probably left their phone somewhere and forgot to bring it with them, but I bet the phone is sitting right in their hand playing an annoying jingle during a quiet seminar. Thanks to these things I can't get a hold of these girls anymore. I wonder if they even have house phones. They probably don't answer them, they let the machine get it. Then that damn robot guy tells me to leave a message after the beep and I just feel like yelling, *"Here's a message for ya, ANSWER YOUR FREAKIN' PHONE!!!"*. Everybody is giving everyone the cold shoulder these days. Nobody has time for anyone. Whatever happened to people getting along and having a good old time? Now everyone wants to start trouble and crash the party.

I don't like it when my date is taller than me. It's tough these days though. Big shoes are in. I'm not that tall either, so that doesn't help. The girl can be 4'11" and be 6'4" after she puts her shoes on. When I take girls to the Drive-In, their heads go right through the sunroof. If you only knew how many girls bumped their heads on the top of my door frame before. My ex told me we didn't see eye to eye. So I went into my shed to find a saw. It was either that or I tied bricks to my shoes.

Women have filing cabinets too. Every single word, phrase, sentence, quote, and story you tell them is being recorded and saved onto a hard drive. Gentlemen (and lesbians), this may be used against you someday if you ever end up in a fight. Whether if it's a few days or a few years later, it'll come back to bite you. Being a guy, I usually don't remember what the heck I even had for breakfast, therefore I either forfeit, surrender, or lose miserably. Most of the time it happens so quickly I don't even remember what we're fighting about. Next thing I know she takes out a tape recorder of me saying something I don't even remember ever saying. I told her, *"Nice try, that's not my voice!"*. The next thing I know she's popping a video in the VCR of me actually saying it. It's unbelievable! They're like secret agents.

Girls say they hate guys who are complete jerks. Two days later they wake up in bed with another complete jerk. Then five minutes later they have the nerve to say guys are confusing. They say they want guys who are romantic. The thing is, us men don't look manly when we're romantic. When we get romantic, you women don't take us seriously anyway. You give us a confused look, like, *"what's the catch?"*. There isn't any catch, you said you wanted a guy who is romantic, I'm being romantic and you look at me like I'm some kind of freak.

Cheerleaders crack me up too. Their boyfriends on the football team are even embarrassed to be seen with them in public.

- *"Hey Mandy, I am going to go on the field now and play football. You can just stay right here on the sidelines and um…show everybody how you can spell the name of our team. Maybe you can even show them how you dance. Better yet, dance and spell at the same time. You'll blow their minds! I'll talk to you later, Baby Cake."*

I really think it's easier to get influenza than it is to get a girlfriend in this country. For you guys who might not be aware, women will trick you. They think they're so sneaky.

- *"If I switched identities with my friend Tina, but was still me on the inside, would you still make love with me?"*

- *"Hell yeah, sure I would honey."*

- *"What are you trying to say? You're attracted to my friend Tina? You like Tina now?!!*

- *"No, no, You said you would still be yourself on the inside, but disguised as Tina, and I'm not*

131

*attracted to you for the person you are on the outside. I'm attracted to the person you are on the inside."*

*- "So you're saying you don't find me attractive on the outside?!?!"*

You just can't win sometimes. Another thing is, girls always think they're fat. It's funny because the ones who are really fat think they're skinny. They'll be wearing a tube top showing off a baker's dozen.

I totally support strippers. They're so much cooler than girlfriends. When you get bored with them you can totally just leave. With girlfriends, you're kind of stuck with them. Girlfriends always give you a hard time. Strippers give you as much time as you need to get hard. It's hard to get a stripper to speak. It's hard to get a girlfriend to shut the heck up. Most girlfriends won't give you another chance, but for the right price a stripper would be more than happy to give you another lap dance. You give a stripper money and she takes her clothes off. You give your girlfriend money and she goes out to buy more clothes to put on.

Girls are always looking for trouble. They always want to argue about something. They have to make statements and show people who's boss. They're the root of most problems and they're so provocative. A guy tells a woman what to do and she throws a fit. Women tell us guys what to do and we jump. The world would have been fine if Eve never told Adam to eat that apple. Adam was doing just fine sitting in the garden eating his beans and berries. Then Eve came along and talked him into eating the apple. I bet he didn't even want to taste the damn thing either. Eve was probably just getting on his nerves.

- "C'mon Adam, try this...its really good!! Adam, are you ignoring me?! I said this apple tastes delicious. Hey, Adam!! Adam, come try this!! Are you even listening to a word I'm saying Adam?!!"

- "No!!! You're so annoying, and to think I gave up one of my ribs for you!!"

- "Oh don't even go there. Don't give me that crap! Just try the apple, okay? I met this serpent and he was like, "Hey baby, try this apple", but I was like, "No way, Jose. God said we can't!", so he was all, "What God don't know won't hurt him."

- "I don't think its a good idea. I don't want this whole thing to blow up in my face."

- "Will you try the apple if I put my breasts in your face?"

*i'M SeRiOuS.*

- *"Alright Eve, you have yourself a deal."*

Stuff hit the fan alright, thanks to her.  Like I said, women are always looking for trouble.

135

## The Big Sleep

For every beginning there is an end. People have ends, not just rear ends, but our life ends. It's part of life. I always wanted to go to a wake and find out the guy isn't really dead yet. He just wakes up, starts coughing up some phlegm, wipes his eyes, get's up and jumps right out of the casket like,

-"Hey guys, so what's the big occasion??"

(everybody in awe as he walks over to his weeping wife)

- *"Hey Honey, why the long face??"*

I think its funny when I hear people say, *"He looks like he's asleep. Oh, he looks so nice. "*. Doesn't everybody look like they're asleep when they're laying on their back with their eyes closed? He looks nice?? No kidding, what is he supposed to look like? Is he supposed to be dressed like a clown with polka-dot pants and a balloon in his hand? Is he supposed to have holes in his shoes with his toes poking out? I think a suit and tie is pretty standard. Then they talk about how lovely the casket is. A pricey box with handles and a corpse inside, how lovely. What ever happened to, *"he was a nice man..."*?

# Wally's Corner

Foods: *pasta, chicken fingers, pizza & wings*

Drinks: *Dr. Pepper, coffee*

Season: *summer*

Colors: *blue, brown, & orange*

Sport: *baseball*

Team: *New York Yankees*

Athletes: *Jason Giambi, Cal Ripken, Jr.*

Game: *chess, fooseball*

City: *Los Angeles, CA.*

Hobby: *collecting movie memorabilia*

Trio: *The Three Stooges*

Movie: *Back to the Future (Trilogy)*

Actor (s): *Jim Carrey, Tom Hanks*

*Wally DiCioccio, Jr.*

Actress: *Jennifer Lopez*

Celebrity: *Hulk Hogan*

TV Show: *Seinfeld*

Bands: *Red Hot Chili Peppers, Led Zeppelin*

Song: *pretty much anything by Zeppelin, "Minor Thing", by R. H. C. P.*

Divas: *Britney Spears, Mandy Moore, J. Lo*

Comedian: *Jerry Seinfeld*

Comedies: *National Lampoon's Christmas Vacation, Naked Gun (Trilogy)*

Comics: *Superman, The Far Side*

Cartoons: *Rocko's Modern Life, Popeye*

Book: *"SeinLanguage", by Jerry Seinfeld*

U.S. President: *Bill Clinton*

Pop Icons: *Elvis Presley, Marilyn Monroe*

## About the Author

Wally DiCioccio, Jr. graduated from Villa Maria College, where he studied Fine Arts. On his free time he enjoys art, illustrating, writing comedy, writing lyrics, and filming movies. Wally DiCioccio, Jr. lives and writes in Buffalo, New York. "I'm Serious" is his first book.

Printed in the United States
18954LVS00001B/110

9 781414 013213